The HUGASAURUS

To all the amazing Pappysaurs who inspire with kindness
(and to one in particular).
R.B.

For Niel, the best hugger I know.
C.C.

ORCHARD BOOKS
First published in Great Britain in 2021 by Orchard Books
First published in paperback in 2021

9 10 8

Text © Rachel Bright 2021
Illustrations © Chris Chatterton 2021

HB ISBN 978 1 40835 614 2
PB ISBN 978 1 40835 615 9

Printed and bound in China

FSC
www.fsc.org
MIX
Paper from
responsible sources
FSC® C104740

Orchard Books
An imprint of Hachette Children's Group
Part of Hodder and Stoughton Limited
Carmelite House, 50 Victoria Embankment,
London EC4Y 0DZ

An Hachette UK Company
www.hachette.co.uk
www.hachettechildrens.co.uk

RACHEL BRIGHT   CHRIS CHATTERTON

The HUGASAURUS

ORCHARD

A little Hugasaurus,
who was feeling very happy,
Skipped off through the ferns
and blew a kiss back to her Pappy.

For today, it was a
SPECIAL DAY.
A day to make
some friends!

A chance to run
and hide-and-seek,
for playing
let's-pretend!

This Hugasaur and Pappysaur had **NEVER** been apart . . .

But out into the world she went with wonder in her heart.

And in the dappled sunlight,
she broke into a run.
It wasn't long before she saw
some others having fun!

"Hello!" she called and gave a wave,
exploding in a grin.
And all the little dinosaurs said,
"Hi! Come here! Join in!"

She greeted every one of them
and told them all her name.

They **PLAYED** and **LAUGHED** so perfectly
at many kinds of game.

And, to start with, it was wonderful,
they all slid down the slide.
BUT... then they started wondering
whose turn it was to hide...

A squabbling was bubbling
and growing up and out.
Those little dinosauruses
began to ROAR
and SHOUT!

"I'LL go first!" said one of them.

"NO, ME!"

replied another.

Then he STOMPED an angry foot,
which scared his little brother!

"I **DON'T** want to play with you!"
a Grumpysaurus cried.

"You're **ALWAYS** spoiling **EVERYTHING!**"
another one replied.

Hugasaurus felt quite lost!

OH DEAR,

OH DEAR!

OH DEAR!

How could she bring the sunshine back?

And chase away the tears?

Just then, a fuzzy platypus,
he waddled up on by.
He paused by Hugasaurus
and looked her in the eye...

"What," he wisely offered,
"would your Pappy say to do?
What makes YOU feel better?
...then you could try that too!"

Well, our little Hugasaurus,
she thought of something snug.
If ever she was sad, her dad
would wrap her in a...

....HUG.

So **THAT** was
what she tried
that day.

She hugged them...

ONE...

BY...

ONE...

And slowly they stopped fighting
and remembered to have fun.
Not only that, but magic spread
amongst those twitching ferns.

The little friends, they hide-and-seeked
and beautifully took turns!

And if a quibble simmered,
they all promised to be gentle.
To be a lot more mindful
(and a lot less accidental!)

Our little Hugasaurus
she had started off some ripples,
And soon those little huggles,
they became some DOUBLE-TRIPLES!

Since when you
choose to shrug it off,
Or maybe **HUG IT OUT**,

There's no need
for all that stomping.
You won't want to
pout or shout!

And in choosing a
NICE DOING,
you might just change
ONE mind.

And that, in turn, might

shape a world...

...where everyone is **KIND**.